Tiara Club

✦ AT RUBY MANSIONS ✦

VIVIAN FRENCH

The Tiara Club

AT RUBY MANSIONS

Princess Chloe
AND THE
Primrose Petticoats

KATHERINE TEGEN BOOKS
HarperTrophy®
An Imprint of HarperCollinsPublishers

The Tiara Club at Ruby Mansions:
Princess Chloe and the Primrose Petticoats
Copyright © 2008 by Vivian French

www.harpercollinschildrens.com

Library of Congress Catalog Card Number: 2007905255
ISBN 978-0-06-143484-6

Typography by Amy Ryan

❖

First U.S. edition, 2008

For the real Princess Chloe,
and her lovely mum, Queen Moira
—V.F.

The Royal Palace Academy
for the Preparation of Perfect Princesses
(Known to our students as "The Princess Academy")

OUR SCHOOL MOTTO:
A Perfect Princess always thinks of others before herself,
and is kind, caring, and truthful.

Ruby Mansions offers a complete education for Tiara Club princesses with emphasis on the creative arts. The curriculum includes:

Innovative Ideas for our Friendship Festival

Designing Floral Bouquets (all thorns will be removed)

Ballet for Grace and Poise

A visit to the Diamond Exhibition
(on the joyous occasion of Queen Fabiola's birthday)

Our principal, Queen Fabiola, is present at all times, and students are in the excellent care of the head fairy godmother, Fairy G., and her assistant, Fairy Angora.

OUR RESIDENT STAFF & VISITING EXPERTS INCLUDE:

KING BERNARDO IV *(Ruby Mansions Governor)*

LADY ARAMINTA *(Princess Academy Matron)*

LADY HARRIS *(Secretary to Queen Fabiola)*

QUEEN MOTHER MATILDA *(Etiquette, Posture, and Flower Arranging)*

We award tiara points to encourage our Tiara Club princesses toward the next level. All princesses who earn enough points at Ruby Mansions will attend a celebration ball, where they will be presented with their Ruby Sashes.

Ruby Sash Tiara Club princesses are invited to go on to Pearl Palace, our very special residence for Perfect Princesses, where they may continue their education at a higher level.

PLEASE NOTE:

Princesses are expected to arrive at the Academy with a *minimum* of:

TWENTY BALL GOWNS
(with all necessary hoops, petticoats, etc.)

TWELVE DAY-DRESSES

SEVEN GOWNS
suitable for garden parties and other special daytime occasions

TWELVE TIARAS

DANCING SHOES
five pairs

VELVET SLIPPERS
three pairs

RIDING BOOTS
two pairs

Cloaks, muffs, stoles, gloves, and other essential accessories, as required

Oh, I'm so excited!

I mean, here we are at Ruby Mansions, learning to be Perfect Princesses. Isn't that just so amazing? And you're here too. Hurray! I'm so glad you can keep us company. I'm Princess Chloe. Have I told you that? You might have met the Rose Room Princesses already—Charlotte, Katie, Daisy, Alice, Sophia, and Emily. I'm in the Poppy Room, and so are Jessica, Georgia, Olivia, Lauren, and Amy, and we're all special friends. We're going to have so much fun!

Chapter One

"What? What's that you say, child?" The new principal had her ear trumpet an inch away from my nose. "Date, you say? What date? It's Monday today. First day of the term!"

I took a deep breath and spoke

as clearly as I could. "Your Majesty, I'm sorry I'm late!"

Queen Fabiola jumped. "My dear!" she said. "There's no need to shout. A Perfect Princess never raises her voice. And why are you late?"

I hung my head. I absolutely

couldn't tell her the real reason.

"I don't know," I mumbled.

"Slow? Your horses were too slow?" Queen Fabiola gave a sort of bark. I think she was laughing. "Dear me. If I've heard that excuse once, I've heard it a thousand times. Well, you're here now, so you'd better run along and find your friends. What did you say your name was?"

"Princess Chloe," I said as loudly as I dared.

"Princess Zoe?" My principal looked puzzled. "I'm sure Princess Zoe arrived earlier. I didn't realize there were two of you. Never mind.

I'll ask Lady Harris to check the lists later. Do you know which dormitory you're in?"

I nodded. It seemed safer than trying to speak.

"Good, good. Run along, then." And Queen Fabiola waved me away with her ear trumpet.

I didn't mean to be late to arrive at Ruby Mansions.

My mother's always busy doing queenly things, so my great-aunt looks after me. And she's very strict. She thinks I should wear plain satin gowns to make me look taller (I'm quite small for my age), but I just *love* flowers and beads and embroidery, and lots and lots of fluffy petticoats. I'm very lucky because I have lots of girl cousins just a little bit older than me. They give me their dresses when they grow out of them, and they're *gorgeous*!

My most favorite dress ever is a beautiful pale forget-me-not blue, with gathered skirts so you can see the petticoats underneath. And would you believe it? The petticoats are covered with tiny yellow primroses. Honestly, when I first saw it I thought I would die of excitement! But do you know what my great-aunt said? She said it was too flowery, and I wasn't allowed to wear it. But I just knew it would be absolutely perfect for the Ruby Mansions First Day of School ball.

And that was why I was late. I had to wait until my great-aunt had gone downstairs to talk to the

coachman. As soon as she'd gone, I
threw open my trunk and squeezed
in my primrose petticoat dress, and
all the other pretty ones as well. It
was a tight fit (I am not very good

at packing!), and there were some papers and cards that got in the way, so I shoved them under my bed. My great-aunt kept calling me to hurry up and come downstairs, but she never guessed what I was doing.

Chapter Two

It took me a while to find my way to the dormitories. I wandered around the hallways a bit, and then I met Fairy G. She was puffing along with a pile of notebooks, but she stopped when she saw me.

"Aha! Princess Chloe!" she said.

"Welcome to Ruby Mansions!"

"Please, Fairy G.," I asked, "can you tell me where the Poppy Room is?"

"Through the glass doors, across the ballroom, and up the stairs at the end," Fairy G. told me. "The

Rose Room is on the right, and the Poppy Room is on the left."

And she beamed and puffed away, dropping things as she went. Fairy G. is the most important Fairy Godmother in the Princess Academy. Sometimes we see her, and sometimes we see her assistant, Fairy Angora, but they both look after us. Fairy G. is a lot of fun. I think she's my favorite teacher.

The stairs wound around and around, but at last I couldn't go any farther. In front of me were two doors. I peeped cautiously inside the first one—and stared. It was so pretty. Roses cascaded over the wallpaper, and there were roses embroidered on the bedspreads. Princesses Charlotte, Katie, Daisy, Alice, Sophia, and Emily were busy unpacking their boxes and trunks, and when they saw me they waved cheerfully.

"Isn't this the most wonderful Rose Room?" Alice said. "Go and see the Poppy Room! You'll love it!"

I hurried next door. It was beautiful. Pink, red, and white poppies were scattered everywhere—even the carpet had a poppy design. And

then I saw my friends piled on a couple of beds at the far end, chatting and laughing.

"Hi!" I called. "I'm here!"

Have you ever been hugged by five friends at once? It was great!

"We were wondering when you'd

arrive," Georgia said. "We were beginning to get worried." And she gave me a little extra hug.

"What do you think of our room?" Olivia asked.

"It's wonderful," I said. "It's not a bit like our room in Silver Towers."

Jessica grinned. "And our new principal isn't a bit like Queen Samantha Joy. Have you met her yet?"

"Yes," I said. "She's really deaf, isn't she? She thinks my name is Princess Zoe."

Lauren and Amy began to giggle. "She thought I was called Mamie, and Lauren was called Maureen!" Amy told me. "We had to show her our invitations before she got it right."

A cold feeling hit my stomach, as if I'd swallowed a lump of ice. "Invitations?" I said feebly.

Georgia jumped up and ran to

her bedside table. She came back waving a gold-embossed card with a huge crown on the top.

As Georgia read it out loud, the ice lump in my stomach grew bigger and bigger as I realized what I'd done. My invitation was mixed up in the papers I'd shoved under my bed!

His Most Royal Highness King Bernardo the Fourth, Governor of Ruby Mansions, wishes to invite Princess Georgia to a ball in his illustrious Gilded Ballroom in order to celebrate the beginning of a new term at Ruby Mansions.

Please keep your invitation and present it on arrival in order to be admitted.

"Chloe! You're all pale!" Olivia said. "Are you all right?"

"No," I said. "I don't have my invitation!"

Chapter Three

My friends told me it wouldn't matter, but I knew it did. It was such a bad way to begin my very first day at Ruby Mansions.

"Go and see Fairy G.," Lauren suggested.

I nodded. "I'll go now."

"I'll come with you," Jessica said, jumping up.

We were crossing the ballroom when we saw Princess Diamonde and Princess Gruella, the horrible twins, coming toward us. Gruella looked very upset. Her eyes were red, and she was blowing her nose.

Even though none of us Poppy Roomers like her very much, we stopped to ask if she was all right.

"No, I'm not." She sniffed. "One of our trunks is missing, and it's got *all* my ball gowns in it!"

"That's *terrible*," I said. "I'm so sorry."

"Have you told Fairy G.?" Jessica asked.

Diamonde tossed her head. "Of course she has. She's not stupid, like *some* people! Come on, Gruella!" And she stormed off, dragging Gruella behind her.

Jessica and I watched them leave. "Why does Diamonde always

have to be so mean?" I asked.

Jessica shrugged. "Who knows? Let's find Fairy G.!"

We went through the ballroom and into the hallway. There were lots of doors, but none of them had names on them.

"Maybe we should just knock on one," Jessica suggested. "Go on, Chloe—choose a door."

I looked around. "That one!" I said, and we marched toward it.

Jessica knocked and a voice called, "Come in."

My heart sank. It was Queen Fabiola—our principal.

Of course we had to go in.

Queen Fabiola was sitting behind a golden desk, and her assistant sat on a small chair beside her.

"Why, it's Princess Jessica and

the second Princess Zoe!" Queen Fabiola looked at me over the top of her glasses. "Lady Harris, I don't think you've met this Princess Zoe."

I began to curtsey to Lady Harris, but I caught my foot and fell over. I felt so silly as I got to my

feet, and Queen Fabiola frowned.

"Really, Princess Zoe! You *must* learn to behave a little more like a Perfect Princess." She pointed her ear trumpet at Jessica and me. "Well? What was it you wanted?"

I didn't know whether to ask where Fairy G. was or to tell her about my invitation, so I said nothing.

"Come along, child—come along!" Queen Fabiola began to tap on her desk.

I gulped. "I'm very sorry, Your Majesty," I said, "but I've lost my invitation to the Ruby Mansions First Day of School ball."

This time, Queen Fabiola looked stern. *Very* stern.

"I can forgive one mistake, Princess Zoe," she said. "I can even forgive two. But you seem determined to get yourself into trouble. I will consider the matter of your missing invitation. Please come back tomorrow morning!"

Chapter Four

I felt awful. And as Jessica and I walked out, Diamonde and Gruella were waiting outside. Diamonde gave us a nasty look.

"In trouble already?" she asked. "Imagine that!"

"So why are *you* here?" Jessica asked.

Gruella made a face. "Fairy G. told me to come and tell Queen Fabiola about my trunk."

"Oh, dear!" I couldn't help feeling sorry for her, even if she wasn't very nice.

"I do hope it arrives in time for the ball," she said—and she sounded really anxious. "Diamonde's got a beautiful dress to wear, but I haven't got anything."

"Couldn't Diamonde lend you one of her other dresses?" Jessica suggested.

Diamonde glared at Jessica. "All

of my other dresses are packed with Gruella's."

"Diamonde made a fuss about her best dress being squashed," Gruella said. "She moaned and

moaned until Mommy packed it in a special box for her."

Diamonde smiled smugly. "You see?" she said. "I was right."

"But I didn't know our trunk was

going to get lost!" Gruella wailed.

"Poor you." I tried to think of a way to make her feel better. "You can have one of my dresses, if you like. I've got tons and tons!"

I knew I'd made a mistake as soon as I finished speaking. I could see from the twins' faces they thought I was being a show-off.

"Thank you, gracious princess," Diamonde said. She sounded very sarcastic.

Gruella sneered. "Who's a lucky little princess?"

"I didn't mean it to sound like that," I began, but it was too late.

Diamonde opened Queen Fabiola's door, and she and Gruella flounced through.

Jessica squeezed my arm. "Just ignore them."

But I couldn't. A part of me really did feel sorry for Gruella. I kept remembering how sad she'd looked in the ballroom, and I *did* know how she must be feeling about the ball. I'd been miserable when I thought I'd have to wear one of my plain satin dresses. It would be terrible to have no dress at all!

When Jessica and I got back to the Poppy Room, we found Lauren waiting for us.

"Hi!" she said cheerfully. "Every-one else has gone down to tea. Have you gotten your invitation?"

I shook my head. "I need to see Queen Fabiola tomorrow morning."

"I'm sure it'll be all right." Lauren patted my arm. "Oh—have you heard? The twins have lost their luggage!"

"We saw them downstairs," Jessica said. "They're just as nasty as ever."

"Gruella might have been grumpy because she hasn't got any ball gowns," I suggested.

"A Perfect Princess always thinks

the best of others," Jessica quoted. "You're a Perfect Princess, Chloe. Come on. We'd better not be late for tea."

After tea was over, we were sent
back to our rooms to unpack our
trunks. I felt so much better when I
pulled out my dress with the primrose petticoats, and all the Poppy

Roomers *oooh*ed and *aaaah*ed in amazement.

"You'll be the belle of the ball!" Olivia told me as I hung my dress on the front of my wardrobe.

"If I'm allowed to go," I said.

"Of course you will be," Georgia said firmly.

There was a knock on the door, and Gruella waltzed in, with Diamonde close behind her. Gruella didn't look upset anymore. She looked as if she was on top of the world.

"I've come to choose my dress," she announced. "The porter took my trunk away by mistake, and it won't arrive here until next week."

As my friends stared in astonish-
ment, Diamonde gave us a sneery
smile. "Aren't we *so* lucky that
Chloe has tons of dresses, and can
spare one for poor little Gruella?"

And then Gruella saw my dress

with the primrose petticoats hanging on my wardrobe. She gave a little gasp, and my stomach lurched.

I just knew what she was going to say—and she said it.

"I'll have that dress." And she marched over to it.

I couldn't move.

"But that's Chloe's special dress for King Bernardo's ball," Amy protested.

Gruella turned around, her eyebrows raised.

"What do you say, Chloe? Can I have this one? After all, you do have tons of them . . ."

"That's right," Diamonde agreed. "Tons and tons! And you *did* say Gruella could have one!"

Chapter Five

What could I say? I had offered Gruella a dress. And it would be horrible to say she couldn't have that one, after I'd sounded so boastful.

I swallowed hard. "That's fine," I said. "I . . . I really hope you enjoy wearing it."

"Oh, I will," Gruella said, and just for a second she looked really happy. And then she, Diamonde, and the dress were gone.

"Wow!" Lauren said loudly. "You're an angel, Chloe. I'd never have let her walk off with my very best dress like that!"

"What are you going to wear to the ball?" Georgia asked.

I sat down on my bed and felt a bit sick. "I'm not sure," I said. "I'll decide tomorrow. When I know whether I'm actually going to go to the ball."

I didn't sleep very well that night. I kept counting all the things that had gone wrong. I'd been late arriving at school, the principal didn't like me and I was too scared to tell her my real name, I might not be allowed to go to King Bernardo's ball, and Gruella had my beautiful primrose petticoat dress.

I told myself a Perfect Princess should be glad she'd done such a good deed, but it didn't make me feel any better. Not one bit.

By the time the alarm bell rang, I was worn out. I crept out of bed, and although Georgia and Jessica tried their best to cheer me up, I couldn't eat any breakfast.

We were about to clear our plates when Fairy G. came sailing into the dining hall.

"Good morning, everybody!" she boomed. "Now, I have to tell

you of a change in arrangements. Queen Fabiola feels that one or two of you have forgotten how to curtsey and how to behave as Perfect Princesses should. She is concerned that you will not appear your best at King Bernardo's ball."

Fairy G. didn't look at me, but I could feel my face burning.

"So, this morning," Fairy G. went on, "we're going to have a dress rehearsal. Run upstairs and put on your ball gowns, and hurry to the ballroom. Queen Fabiola and I will meet you there."

Everyone was thrilled—except me. We all flew up to our rooms, and by the time I walked slowly into the Poppy Room it was a froth of skirts and petticoats.

"What are you going to wear, Chloe?" Jessica was struggling with her sash, and Lauren was helping

her. They both looked fabulous.
Jessica had the loveliest dress covered
in sparkly silver stars, and Lauren
was wearing the most beautiful pink
velvet.

I went to my wardrobe. I'd

packed my pretty dresses so badly they were all wrinkled, and looked terrible. I pulled out one of the satin dresses instead.

When I put it on, I looked in the mirror and I nearly cried. Everyone else had stars or sparkles or lace, and my dress was so plain. It was too big, as well—my great-aunt thought it would last longer that way.

"You look very pretty," Georgia said, but I knew she was just being nice.

Chapter Six

The ballroom was already full of princesses when we arrived, and I felt worse and worse. Queen Fabiola was standing on a platform at one end, and Fairy G. boomed at us to hurry up. I tried to sneak into the back row, but Queen

Fabiola waved me over.

"Ah! Princess Zoe! Come to the front. I'm particularly anxious about you. I want to see if it's possible for you to curtsey without falling over."

Of course that made me even

more nervous. Fairy G. gave me an encouraging wink, but I couldn't smile back.

"Let us begin," Queen Fabiola ordered. "Step right, left foot behind, head up, and curtsey! Oh, *excellent*, Princess Olivia! *Enchanting*, Princess Gruella!" She paused, and I thought she was going to scold me again, but she was looking past me. "Come here, Gruella my dear. Perhaps you and Olivia could demonstrate how a curtsey should be performed!"

And there was Gruella—in my dress with the primrose petticoats— pushing her way to the front. She and Olivia turned to face us, and as they turned their backs on Fairy G. and Queen Fabiola I saw Fairy G.'s eyes open wide. Queen Fabiola began to speak—then she stopped and stared.

"Gruella, my dear child! Your dress! It's truly lovely, but it isn't buttoned up." She peered more closely at it. "Didn't you tell me your ball gowns had been lost? Where has this dress come from? It does seem a little too small for you . . ."

Before Gruella could say anything, Olivia dropped yet another of her brilliant curtsies. "Excuse me, Your Majesty," she said, and her voice was very clear. "Princess Chloe lent it to her. It's Chloe's very best dress, but she felt so sorry for

Princess Gruella, she said she could wear it."

Queen Fabiola looked pleased, but confused. "How kind of Princess Chloe," she said. "That is a truly generous gesture." She gazed over

my head at the princesses behind me. "Will Princess Chloe please step forward?"

I took a deep breath, stepped forward, and sank into my very best curtsey.

"What's this? What? *What?*" Our principal looked so muddled that Fairy G. took pity on her.

"I think," she boomed, "there has been some confusion. This is Princess Chloe, Your Majesty, and she is, as I know well, the kindest of princesses. I would also suggest there has been some confusion about the dresses."

Fairy G. winked at me and

waved her wand.

The air was so filled with sparkly fairy dust we all began to sneeze. When we'd stopped sneezing, there I was in my wonderful dress with

the primrose petticoats, and Gruella was wearing my satin dress! And do you know what? She looked absolutely beautiful! Every princess in the ballroom began to

clap, and Queen Fabiola waved her ear trumpet at me.

"Well done, Princess Chloe. And I do apologize for calling you by the wrong name, my dear. Lady Harris, could we find Princess Chloe an invitation to King Bernardo's ball?"

Lady Harris smiled at me. "Of course," she said.

Chapter Seven

$\mathcal{K}$ing Bernardo's First Day of School ball was fabulous! We were taken there in the Ruby Mansions coaches, which are gold, with the most plush ruby-red velvet cushions.

King Bernardo took our

invitations and then kissed our hands—and he told me I looked beautiful! I blushed bright red, but I didn't care. I was wearing my

dress with the primrose petticoats,
and I was with my best friends.
We danced and danced!

When the coaches came to take us home, Diamonde and Gruella were in our coach, and Gruella actually smiled at me.

"Thank you for the dress," she said.

"You look wonderful in it," I said, and I meant every word. "Please keep it."

"Okay," Gruella said, and she gave me a funny little sideways look. "I'll say yes, because I know you've got tons and tons of other dresses."

And I still don't know if she was being sly or not. But I don't mind, because Ruby Mansions is fantastic—and I'm so happy here.

I'll see you soon!

What happens next?

FIND OUT IN

Princess Jessica
✧ AND THE ✧
Best-Friend Bracelet

Hi! It's me—Princess Jessica! And it's lovely to meet you, and to know you're here at Ruby Mansions with me and my friends from the Poppy Room. Have you met us all? There's Chloe, Olivia, Lauren, Georgia, Amy, and me. And Charlotte, Katie, Daisy, Alice, Sophia, and Emily are in the Rose Room right next door to us. Things would be just about perfect if only those horrible twins, Diamonde and Gruella, weren't here. They get worse and worse—especially Diamonde!

Visit all your favorite

The Tiara Club

Go to www.tiaraclubbooks.com

Tiara Club princesses!

The Tiara Club
AT SILVER TOWERS

for games, puzzles, and more fun!

You are cordially invited
to the Royal Princess Academy!

Introducing the new class of princesses
at Ruby Mansions

Katherine Tegen Books
An Imprint of HarperCollinsPublishers

HarperTrophy®
An Imprint of HarperCollinsPublishers